I0867439

On the Tracks

John Allan

HUNGRY TOMATO™

Copyright © 2021 Hungry Tomato Ltd

First published in Great Britain in 2021 by Hungry Tomato Ltd
F1, Old Bakery Studios
Blewetts Wharf
Malpas Road, Truro
Cornwall, TR1 1QH, UK

No part of this publications may be reproduced, stored in a retrieval system, or transmitted in any form or by any means, electronic, mechanical, photocopying, recording, or otherwise, without the prior written permission of the copyright owner.

A CIP catalog record for this book is available from the British Library

ISBN 978 1 913440 67 1

Manufactured in the USA

Discover more at
www.hungrytomato.com

Contents

Words that appear in **bold** are explained in the glossary

The Mighty Mechanics

Shovels are often used to clear snow from the tracks.

We are the **Mighty Mechanics.** Welcome to our **workshop**. We work on some amazing vehicles, and here are a few of the **tools** we use to fix them.

Maglev Trains

This is the Shanghai **Maglev** train. It is the fastest train in the world with a top speed of 267 mph (430 km/h).

Maglev trains don't have wheels, they use magnets to lift the trains off the tracks and move them at incredible speeds.

Its design makes it almost impossible for the train to come off the tracks

This is the view the driver has when speeding through a tunnel.

They are fast, quiet and friendly to the environment.

Takabisha Roller Coaster

The **Takabisha** in Japan, is the steepest roller coaster in the world. The ride starts with an amazing drop, where the rider is almost upside down.

This high speed coaster, reaches 62 mph (100 km/h) in 2 seconds.

The ride starts with a vertical lift of 141 feet (43 meters).

The first drop is very, very steep!

Riders are sped through loops and turned upside down 7 times!

Bobsleigh

Bobsleigh is a **winter sport**, where teams make timed runs down narrow, twisting, icy tracks, on specially designed sleds.

Teams have either 2 or four members. This is a two person bobsleigh.

Teams can reach speeds of over 75 mph (120 km/h).

While racing, the team keep their bodies tucked inside the sleigh, making them more **streamlined.**

After a strong starting push, the bobsleigh is kept speeding along by **gravity.**

Bullet Trains

This is the original **bullet train**, the Japanese **Shinkansen**. It gets its name for its speed and because the front looks like a bullet.

Unlike a maglev, these superfast trains run on wheels.

This is a French bullet train. They hold the record for the fastest train with wheels, reaching 357 mph (574 km/h).

When these trains exit tunnels at speed, you can hear a sudden boom, which sounds like they have broken the **sound barrier**.

Mallard Steam Train

Steam trains have been running for over 200 years but are now used for **transport** much less than they were in the past.

The Mallard holds the world speed record for a steam **locomotive,** having reached 126 mph (203 km/h).

This is the Mallard 60009 Union of South Africa, which stopped running in 2014.

The locomotive is operated by the driver and a fireman, who feeds coal into the engine to power it.

Skeleton and Luge Racing

In both these winter sports, riders race down the same ice tracks as bobsleighs.

The skeleton has a single rider, who races head first down the track!

The top speed for a skeleton is 80.3 mph (129.2 km/h)

In the luge, riders race feet first, on their back.

The top speed recorded for a luge is 101.9 mph (164 km/h).

There are no brakes. Riders stop by dragging their feet on the ground.

Superman Roller Coasters

Superman roller coasters are named after the famous **superhero** because they make you feel like you are flying through the air.

There are several Superman coasters around the world.

These roller coasters are made from very strong steel.

Superman: Ultimate Flight was the first roller coaster to have a pretzel shaped loop.

Superman: Escape from Krypton, in California can reach a top speed of 100 mph (161 km/h), in about 7 seconds.

Bulldog Tank

Tanks aren't usually speedy, because they are very heavy. The **Walker Bulldog** was much lighter than most tanks and is still one of the fastest tanks ever.

This is the M1a2 Abrams tank. At 70 tons, it is much heavier than the Bulldog!

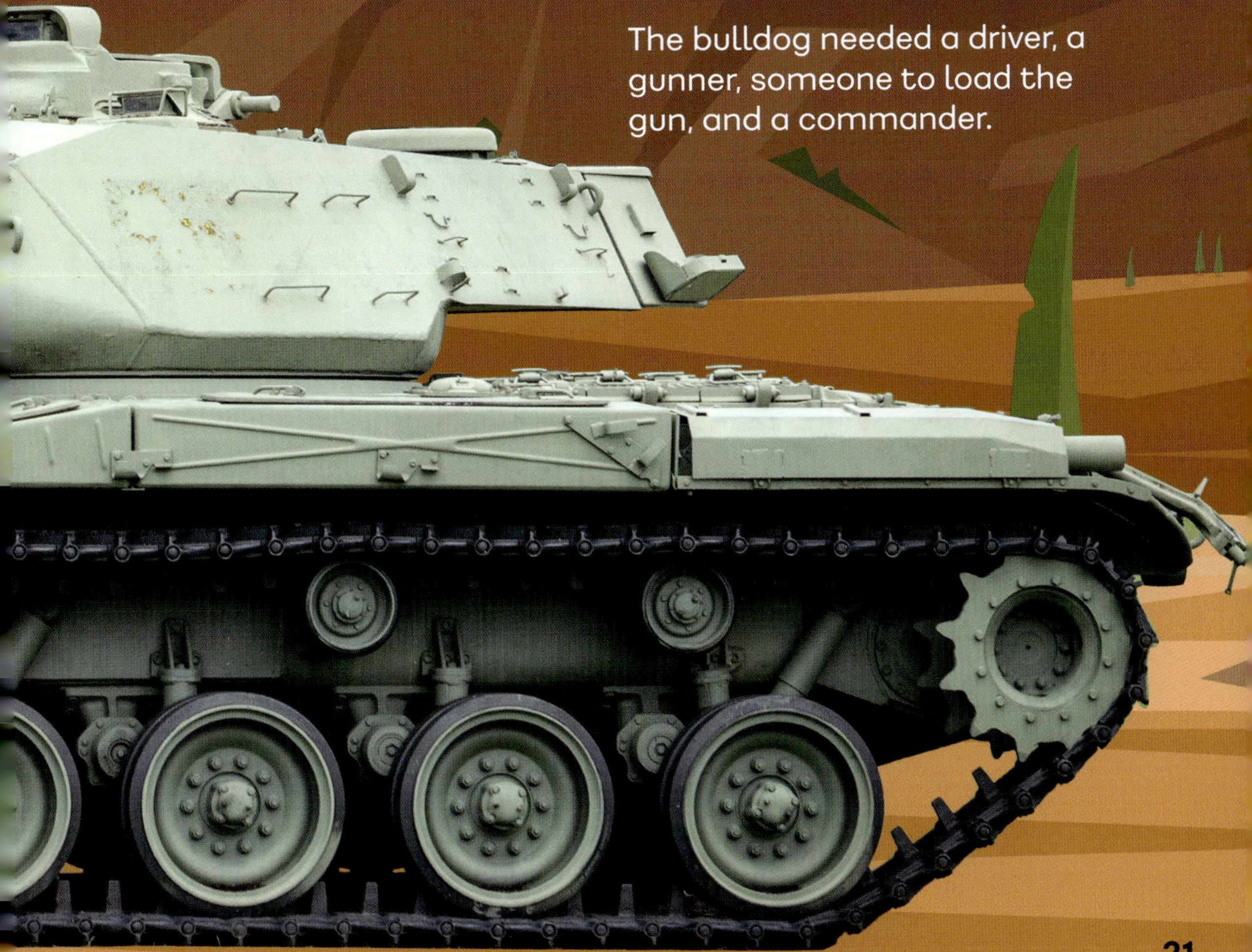

The bulldog needed a driver, a gunner, someone to load the gun, and a commander.

Snowmobiles

Snowmobiles also run on caterpillar tracks. They were designed for winter travel but are now used for sport as well.

Racing snowmobiles can sometimes reach speeds of 200 mph (320 km/h.)

Spiky treads help to stop it slipping in the snow.

Snowmobilers don't just race on snow. Some races take place across grass, ice and other surfaces.

Some snowmobiles have skis on the front for steering.

Glossary

gravity the force that pulls objects towards the center of the Earth.

locomotive a railway vehicle or engine that pulls a train.

maglev a train which glides along a track, supported and moved by magnets.

sound barrier is the speed that sound travels at.

streamlined something with smooth lines, which can move through air easily, making it go faster.

transport to take people or items from one place to another on a vehicle.

Measuring Speed

A vehicle's speed is usually measured in either **miles per hour (mph)** or **kilometers per hour (km/h).**

1 mph = 1.6 km/h

Picture Credits
(abbreviations: t = top; b = bottom; m = middle; l = left; r = right; bg = background)

Alex Churilov 5bl; Alongkorn Naranong 9ml; Andrew Rybalko (mechanics illustrations); Artur Didyk 1m, 16m; ChameleonsEye 2m, 18m; cyo bo 6m; Dainis Derics 17t; Droidworker 1bg, 10bg, 16bg; Ihor Biliavskyi 20bg; Iurii Osadchi 10m, 11t; JS Rowley 15tr; Kapuska 8m; Karolis Kavolelis 21t; Konstantin Zaykov 23t; Lilkin 22m; Malika Keehl 2bg, 18bg; MicroOne 12bg; Miracel vaart 6bg; olrat 13t; Peter Austin 14m; Pit Stock 19t; Piti Sirisriro 12m; Pixel-Shot 5bm; PrimaStockPhoto 4br; SlaSla 22bg; ssuaphotos 7tr;TOM.RUETHAI 20m; VikiVector 4bg; VVadyab Pico 8bg, 14bg, 24bg.

Every effort has been made to trace the copyright holders and we apologise in advance for any unintentional omissions. We would be pleased to insert the appropriate acknowledgement in any subsequent edition of this publication.